HEY, AL

Story by Arthur Yorinks

Pictures by Richard Egielski

Farrar, Straus and Giroux

New York

Text copyright © 1986 by Arthur Yorinks
Pictures copyright © 1986 by Richard Egielski
All rights reserved
Library of Congress catalog card number: 86-80955
Published simultaneously in Canada by Collins Publishers, Toronto
Color separations by Offset Separations Corp.
Printed in the United States of America by The John D. Lucas Printing Company
Bound by A. Horowitz and Sons
Typography by Cynthia Krupat
First edition, 1986
Second printing, 1987

For Adrienne,
Syd and Bongo
A.Y.

For my mother and father
R.E.

AL, a nice man, a quiet man, a janitor, lived in one room on the West Side with his faithful dog, Eddie. They ate together. They worked together. They watched TV together. What could be bad?

Plenty.

"Look at this dump!" Eddie growled. "We can't have a house? A little back yard to run around in for a change?"

"Oh, sure," Al snapped. "Today it's a house you want. Tomorrow, who knows? Maybe the moon!"

"The moon? *The moon?*" Eddie howled. "Pigeons live better than us!"

No, life wasn't easy for Al and Eddie. They were always working, always struggling. It was always something.

One morning, while Al was shaving, a voice called to him. "Hey, Al," it said. Al turned and saw a bird. A large bird.

"Al," said the bird, "are you working too hard? Still struggling and going nowhere? *Hmmm?* Listen. Have I got a place for you. No worries, no cares—it's terrific."

"Huh?" Al said. He was confused.

"Al, Al, *Al!* You need a change. Tomorrow, come and be my guest. Eddie, too. You'll see, you'll *love* it!"

Then, with a few flaps, the bird was gone.

You can imagine that evening's conversation. Eddie was already packing.

"*What?* Just quit my job?" Al said.

"There's more to life than mops and pails!" Eddie insisted.

"But—"

"That's it, we're going. I don't want to hear another word."

At dawn, they were both in the bathroom. Waiting.

The large bird appeared, and Al and Eddie

were ferried thousands of feet upward to an island in the sky.

Unbelievable! Lush trees, rolling hills, gorgeous grass. Birds flitted to and fro. Waterfalls cascaded into shimmering pools.

"Would you look at this view!" Eddie said.
"WOW!" said Al.

Birds sang and brought them food. They ate. They drank. They swam.
They sunbathed. They never had it so good.

"So, Al, is this so terrible?" the large bird asked.

"What a life," Al cooed. "A guy could live like this forever."

The days passed blissfully. As memories of their old life slowly faded, Al and Eddie decided that this was ecstasy.

But ripe fruit soon spoils.

One morning Al woke up and shrieked. "Eddie! Look at us! We're turning into birds!"

Indeed. Their eyes were a little beady, their noses a bit beak-like.

"We've got to get out of here," he croaked. Wings sprouted. Tail feathers plumed.

"Take us back, take us back!" Eddie quacked. "I don't want to be a bird!"

"I'd rather mop floors!" he honked as they both flapped furiously and rose into the air.

"Eddie, be careful, follow me," Al squawked. But Eddie, in a frenzy, was flying in circles, higher and higher.

Exhausted, straining to stay aloft, he plunged into the open sea and was gone.

Al barely made it home in one piece. Alone, without his friend, he was heartbroken.

But, fortunately, Eddie was a talented swimmer, and in no time he found his way back to the West Side.

"Eddie!" Al cried.

"Oh, Al . . ."

Paradise lost is sometimes Heaven found.